D1070965

Remembering Mom's Kubbat Halab

Medeia Sharif

illustrated by
Paran Kim

Albert Whitman & Company
Chicago, Illinois

Bushra missed her dayik—her mom.
So did her brother, Sherzat.

Mom had helped Bushra with math and Sherzat with science.

She was no longer there to tuck them into bed or read to them at night.

They also hadn't eaten their favorite meal since Mom died.

Bushra remembered Mom's kubbat halab, the rice-and-potato patties she had always cooked to golden perfection.

Bushra didn't eat meat, so Mom would make the kubbat halab without filling.

She remembered the soft inside. She remembered the crunchy outside.

Bushra's heart ached when she thought about Mom and her kubbat halab.

Dad was not the best cook even though he tried.
His grilled cheese sandwiches weren't melted enough.
His peanut butter sandwiches were mostly bread.
His soups were thick and salty.

Sherzat and Bushra made faces when they tasted his food.
Bushra got mad sometimes. "Dad, this tastes bad."
"I wish I could cook better, and I wish I could make kubbat halab for you," Dad said.

Bushra visited Grandma after school one day.

Mom used to cook after school. She would sing along to the
radio as she shaped the patties. Bushra missed those days.

"I make the best kubbat halab," Grandma said. She placed the kubbat halab on a fancy round plate that she used for family dinners.

But Grandma's kubbat halab was white, not golden at all.

It was too soft, with no flavor.

It wasn't the same.

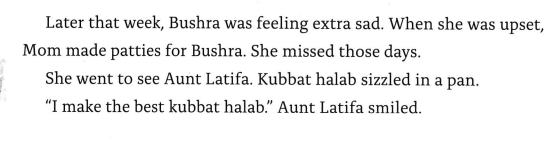

Later that week, Bushra was feeling extra sad. When she was upset,
Mom made patties for Bushra. She missed those days.

She went to see Aunt Latifa. Kubbat halab sizzled in a pan.

"I make the best kubbat halab." Aunt Latifa smiled.

Aunt Latifa dipped a patty in hot mustard, her favorite sauce.
The patties were crispy and hard.

Her kubbat halab reminded Bushra of potato chips.

It wasn't the same.

Bushra went with Dad to restaurants, but they could not find good kubbat halab.

Sherzat tried to help, but he couldn't find websites for places that delivered kubbat halab.

They visited Mom's favorite Middle Eastern grocery store.

There were snacks, but no kubbat halab.

Then Bushra had an idea.

She looked through pictures of Mom cooking.
She realized she had watched Mom cook kubbat halab hundreds of times.
She asked Dad to buy the ingredients.

Bushra showed Dad and Sherzat step-by-step how Mom made kubbat halab.

They boiled the rice,

mashed the potatoes,

and shaped the rice and potatoes into patties.

Then they dipped the patties into a bowl of raw, beaten egg.

Dad fried the patties.

"Baba, flip them over now," Bushra said, remembering how long Mom would wait for each side to brown.

"Sherzat, cover that plate with a napkin so Dad can put the patties on it to drain the grease."
The spicy smell was familiar and comforting.
It reminded her of Mom.

They sat together with the kubbat halab.

Bushra grabbed one of the meatless ones and bit into it.

It was soft inside and crispy outside. It had just the right amount of salt and spices.

But it still wasn't Mom's kubbat halab.

Bushra burst into tears.

"It is okay to cry." Sherzat sniffled. "I cry all the time."

"Your dayik will always be with us." Dad rubbed her back. "And we'll always remember her, especially when we cook together."

Bushra believed them and stopped crying.
She thought about Mom every day, and the
memories were always sweet.

From then on, Bushra and Dad made Mom's kubbat halab all the time. It didn't taste quite the same, but Bushra loved thinking about Mom while they cooked.

They made Mom's other recipes too.
Dad became a better cook. So did Bushra and Sherzat.

Every night Bushra could feel her dayik watching...

Watching Bushra cook with Dad. Watching Bushra eat. Watching Bushra remember her.

Bushra looked upward to the ceiling as if Mom could hear her. And she said with a smile, "We both make the best kubbat halab now."

About Kubbat Halab

Kubbat halab is an Iraqi dish. It is named after Halab, the Arabic name for the Syrian city Aleppo. Aleppo is famous for its many kubba dishes. I have an Iraqi Kurdish background and often ate kubbat halab as a child. It is a rice and potato patty, usually with a ground beef or lamb filling. My mother would also make it without the filling for me. The patty can be shaped like an egg or a small pancake.

My Recipe

Because I'm a vegan—someone who doesn't eat meat, dairy, or eggs—I make my kubbat halab differently than what is described in this book. Although I've used plant-based "ground beef," I prefer making kubbat halab without any filling. The following recipe makes about four patties, so double or triple the amount if you want to make more. Ask an adult to help you with this recipe.

- 1 cup mashed potato flakes (or boiled potato chunks)
- 1 cup cooked jasmine or basmati rice (salted, without oil)
- 2 tablespoons parsley flakes
- 2 tablespoons nutritional yeast (optional)
- 1 VeganEgg (or similar egg replacement)
- sesame or grape-seed oil (see below for amount)

Place the potato, rice, parsley, and nutritional yeast into a medium-sized mixing bowl.

Prepare the VeganEgg according to the label's directions.

Pour the VeganEgg into the bowl and mix everything together with your hands. The VeganEgg will make the mixture moist, but you should have a bowl of water nearby in case the mixture needs a little more liquid. The mixture should stick together without crumbling when handling it.

Dip your hands into the bowl of water so the mixture won't stick to them, and then shape the mixture into flat patties. The thickness of the patties depends on your preference.

Add enough oil to a frying pan to cover the sides of the patties. Set the heat to medium high. Once the oil is hot, place the patties in the pan and deep-fry them on one side. When they are golden, flip them over. When both sides are golden, the patties are done.

Enjoy kubbat halab on their own or with a sauce. I eat the patties with ketchup. They're also good with hot sauce or sweet-and-sour sauce.

To my mom, for her love and inspiration—MS

For my mom, Gyeong-Suk Baek,
who supports me with endless love—PK

Library of Congress Cataloging-in-Publication data
is on file with the publisher.
Text copyright © 2022 by Medeia Sharif
Illustrations copyright © 2022 by Albert Whitman & Company
Illustrations by Paran Kim
First published in the United States of America in 2022
by Albert Whitman & Company
ISBN 978-0-8075-6932-0 (hardcover)
ISBN 978-0-8075-6933-7 (ebook)
All rights reserved. No part of this book may be reproduced or
transmitted in any form or by any means, electronic or mechanical,
including photocopying, recording, or by any information storage and
retrieval system, without permission in writing from the publisher.
Printed in China
10 9 8 7 6 5 4 3 2 1 WKT 26 25 24 23 22

Design by Rick DeMonico

For more information about Albert Whitman & Company,
visit our website at www.albertwhitman.com.